The Strange Adventures of Blue Dog

Jean Van Leeuwen / illustrated by Marco Ventura

Dial Books for Young Readers New York

Published by Dial Books for Young Readers
A division of Penguin Putnam Inc.
345 Hudson Street
New York, New York 10014

Designed by Nancy R. Leo-Kelly
Printed in Hong Kong on acid-free paper
First Edition
1 3 5 7 9 10 8 6 4 2

Library of Congress Cataloging in Publication Data
Van Leeuwen, Jean.
The strange adventures of Blue Dog / by Jean Van Leeuwen;
illustrated by Marco Ventura.—1st ed.
p.   cm.
Summary: Billy's love for his toy Blue Dog, who lives on a toy farm,
transforms both their lives, making Blue Dog's world seem real
and inspiring Billy to get a real dog.
ISBN 0-8037-1878-0
[1. Dogs—Fiction. 2. Toys—Fiction. 3. Farm life—Fiction.]
I. Ventura, Marco, ill. II. Title.
PZ7.V3273St 1999   [E]—dc21   98-26232   CIP   AC

The art was prepared using oil paint on gessoed Fabriano paper.

To my great Aunt Ruthie, who gave me books

J. V. L.

To my wife, Laura, and our daughter Anna

M. V.

Blue Dog lived on a farm.

It was a small farm, just a barn and a chicken coop and a square fenced-in corral. Besides Blue Dog, there were two horses, a spotted cow and her calf, three sheep, and a pig. Six hens and a rooster lived in the chicken coop.

·(·(·(·(·(·(·(·(·

Life was quiet on the farm. Except when Big Billy came to visit.

Big Billy hitched the horses to the wagon, loaded up the calf, and hauled it away. Sometimes he forgot to bring it back, which upset the cow considerably. He put the pig in the hayloft and the rooster on the barn roof and Blue Dog in the chicken coop, where the hens all looked at him strangely.

Things were always in a state of confusion when Big Billy left.

·☽·☽·☽·☽·☽·☽·☽·

One day Big Billy did an even stranger thing. He lifted Blue Dog up, over the chicken coop, over the barn, higher and higher. Big Billy's fingers opened. All Blue Dog could see was hair and pink cheeks and a giant eye.

"I wish I had a dog just like you," Big Billy said softly.

It was an odd feeling to be held and smiled at like that. More nice than scary. When Big Billy put him down again, next to the sheep, Blue Dog felt a little tremble of disappointment.

·☾·☾·☾·☾·☾·☾·☾·☾·

After that Blue Dog often took rides in the warm cup of Big Billy's hand. He played on soft rugs. He went traveling, by land, sea, and air. One day he went farther than ever before, and for the first time saw bright sky and felt the sun and smelled the sweet greenness of grass.

·☾·☾·☾·☾·☾·☾·☾·☾·

But at night Blue Dog always returned to the quiet farm.

Early one morning Blue Dog felt himself first lifted up, then tumbling down into a deep, dark soft-lined hole.

"Today I am taking you to school," said Big Billy's voice.

And the hole began to move.

·☽·☽·☽·☽·☽·☽·☽·☽·

All day it stayed in motion. Blue Dog heard sounds: clanks and whispers, squeaks and shouts. His nose twitched with new smells. But he could not see anything. Until finally Big Billy's fingers closed around him and brought him up to the light.

So this was school.

More Big Billys of different shapes and sizes looked down at him.

"Who is that?" asked one.

"He is my pet," answered Big Billy.

"But he's not real."

"No." The word was full of sorrow.

·☾·☾·☾·☾·☾·☾·☾·☾·

That night Blue Dog did not go back to the farm. He slept in the palm of Big Billy's hand, the fingers curled over him like a blanket.

The moon rose. A soft beam of light reached down from the sky, coming to rest on Big Billy's pillow. Big Billy sighed. And suddenly Blue Dog felt the room flooded with longing.

·☽·☽·☽·☽·☽·☽·☽·☽·

Not many days after that, Blue Dog went on his longest journey yet. It was so long that he stopped wondering where it would end and just took a nap in the soft darkness.

·☾·☾·☾·☾·☾·☾·☾·☾·

When he awoke, they had stopped. There was noise, and the strongest, strangest, sweetest smell.

"Let me out of here!" called Blue Dog.

Then he was blinking in the sunlight. Blinking at a barn so tall, it filled the sky. A chicken coop and a square fenced-in corral. Horses, cows, sheep, pigs, chickens. Even a dog with a white waving tail like a flag. Blue Dog came close to bursting with excitement. A real farm.

Hay. That was the smell that tickled his nose.

Big Billy and Blue Dog lay in it. They rolled in it. They climbed into the hayloft and slid, laughing, down it. They watched horses grazing and cows milking. Pigs wallowing in mud. The dog herding sheep. Chickens clucking and pecking everywhere. Blue Dog was amazed. So much was happening at the real farm.

On the way home he slept, tired but happy, in a pocket full of hay.

·☾·☾·☾·☾·☾·☾·☾·☾·

What happened next seemed like a dream. Blue Dog was falling. Out of his warm sleep into something wet. The wet was sloshing and splashing like a stormy sea. And making the most tremendous noise.

"Help!" Blue Dog struggled to keep his head above water. But the current was strong, dragging him down.

He was tossed and tumbled. Up he bobbed. Down, and up again. He was growing so tired. Then the noise switched to a loud hum. And everything began to spin.

Blue Dog had no thought left except Big Billy.

"Help!" he cried. "Oh, please come and save me."

Miraculously then everything stopped. Fingers plucked him from the swirling water, cradling him safe and sound. Fingers stroked his neck and ears oh so gently. Big Billy.

·☽·☽·☽·☽·☽·☽·☽·☽·

"My pet," he heard just before he fell into sleep.

That night while they both slept, a silvery finger of moonlight poked through the curtains. For just a moment it touched Blue Dog, then moved on to the sleeping farm. And something wondrous and strange quivered in the night air.

The sun streaming in woke Blue Dog the next morning. What was that smell? Could he still be dreaming?

Opening his eyes, he blinked in surprise at the farm. Hay was everywhere. The delicious smell and tickle of it filled the barn. It overflowed the hayloft. It drifted into the corral, nearly covering the chicken coop.

Blue Dog breathed in hay until he was filled up inside. For the first time his farm seemed real.

•☾•☾•☾•☾•☾•☾•☾•☾•

It seemed even more real when Big Billy came to visit. Big Billy put the horses out to graze. He milked the cow and fed the chickens. And set Blue Dog to herding the sheep and the pig.

Herding was hard work, and the pig refused to budge. Still, Blue Dog went to sleep happy that night.

A real farm, he said to himself over and over, marveling at the thought.

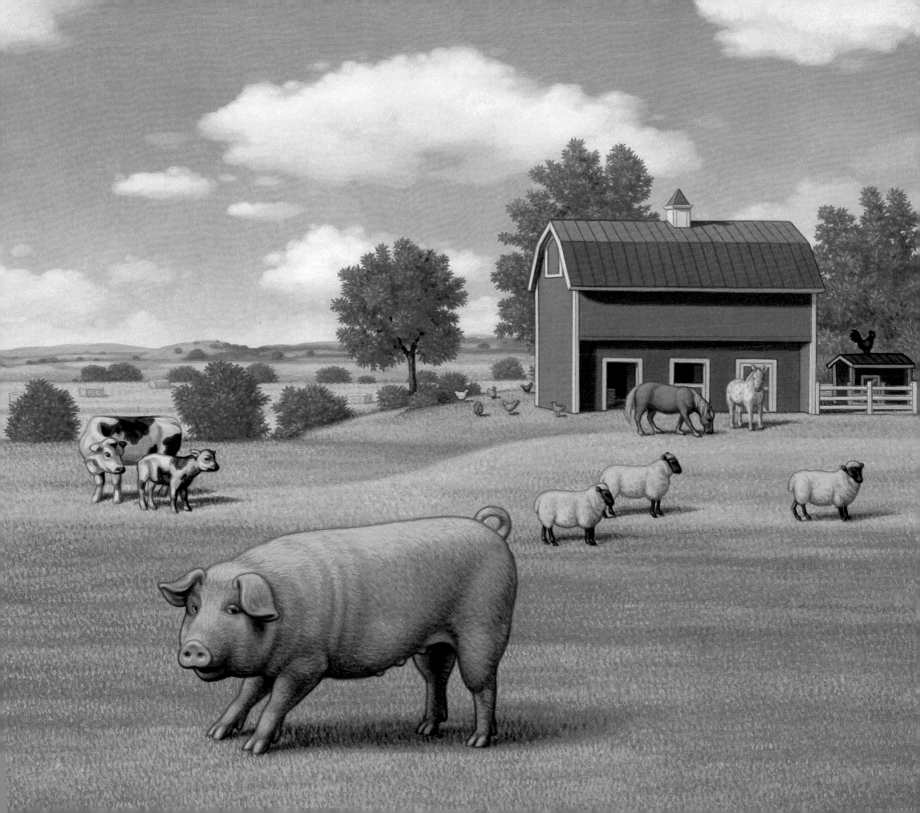

It was the very next day that the dog came to live at Big Billy's house. It was a huge fearsome thing, all tongue and wagging tail and trouble. Big Billy smiled his broadest smile, and kept on smiling. And named his dog Blue.

Now it was Blue who waited for Big Billy to come home from school, and Blue who went traveling. While high up on a shelf, out of reach of his snuffling nose, Blue Dog took care of the farm.

He was happy in his work, except for the silly pig.

·☾·☾·☾·☾·☾·☾·☾·☾·

And when the day was over, Big Billy's fingers would close warmly around him. Up, up he would go, over the chicken coop, over the barn, until he came to rest on Big Billy's pillow.

·☾·☾·☾·☾·☾·☾·☾·☾·

And the two of them slept, while the moon smiled down.
Big Billy and Blue Dog.

•☾•☾•☾•☾•☾•☾•☾•☾•